For Author and his Muse

COWBOY PUG

The Dog Who Rode for Glory

LAURA JAMES

illustrated by ÉGLANTINE CEULEMANS

a

BLOOMSBURY

LONDON   OXFORD   NEW YORK   NEW DELHI   SYDNEY

Bloomsbury Publishing, London, Oxford, New York, New Delhi and Sydney

First published in Great Britain in May 2017 by Bloomsbury Publishing Plc
50 Bedford Square, London WC1B 3DP

www.bloomsbury.com

BLOOMSBURY is a registered trademark of Bloomsbury Publishing Plc

A CIP catalogue record for this book is available from the British Library

ISBN 978 1 4088 6638 2

All papers used by Bloomsbury Publishing are natural, recyclable products made
from wood grown in well managed forests. The manufacturing processes
conform to the environmental regulations of the country of origin

Printed in China by Leo Paper Products, Heshan, Guangdong

3 5 7 9 10 8 6 4 2

Chapter 1

It was an ordinary morning at No. 10, The Crescent. Pug was sunning himself in the front garden while Lady Miranda exercised her faithful steed, Pony.

'Whoa there, boy!' Lady Miranda steadied Pony as she scanned the

horizon. 'Bandits at half past two!' she exclaimed.

Pug didn't know much but that didn't sound good. He took cover.

Pony pawed the ground and shook his mane. The bandits were still a way off, due west of the rose bed, but neither horse nor rider was in the mood for hanging around. Lady Miranda shortened her reins and scooped up her trusty sidekick. Pony was alert and ready. On her command, they charged.

'Yeeee haw!' They galloped towards the bandits. She and Pony were a terrifying sight but the terrain was rocky and, in an unfortunate moment, Pony lost his footing.

'Aaaaargh!'

Horse, rider and passenger came crashing to the earth.

Oooof!

Wendy, Running Footman Will and Running Footman Liam came rushing out of the house. Pug padded over to Lady Miranda, concern showing on his wrinkled face.

'Is everything all right, m'Lady?' asked Wendy, Lady Miranda's housekeeper.

'Wendy, look at Pony,' Lady Miranda replied in anguish. 'I think he's gone ... lame.'

Pug agreed. It didn't look good.

'Running Footman Will, Running Footman Liam, bring the first-aid kit quickly,' Lady Miranda ordered as Pug comforted Pony. 'We might be able to save him.'

It didn't take them long to bandage Pony (who was a very good patient).

When Lady Miranda gave Pony the all-clear they led him back to his stable for a rest.

'Well, that's a relief,' sighed Wendy. 'All's well that ends well, that's what I say.'

'But this isn't the end,' Lady Miranda protested. 'This is only the beginning. What if the bandits come back to kidnap Pug?'

This was not something that Pug had thought of.

'I need a new horse and I need one now!' Lady Miranda declared, sliding her hand across the brim of her hat. 'Running Footman Will, Running Footman Liam, fetch the sedan chair, we're going horse-trading.'

Chapter 2

In no time they were cantering through the busy streets. Inside the sedan chair the bumpy ride made Pug's cowboy hat slip down over his eyes, so he decided it was a good opportunity for a much needed nap. Lady Miranda wouldn't have noticed but for the quiet snore that escaped him.

'Pug!' she nudged him. 'Wake up. We're here.'

They had arrived at some very fine-looking riding stables.

Running Footman Will and Running Footman Liam dropped the sedan chair and Lady Miranda clambered out with Pug under her arm.

Pug sniffed the air. It certainly didn't smell like Pony's stable did.

Lady Miranda gently put Pug on the ground and went to find out who was in charge. Pug waited patiently and was happily daydreaming about jam tarts when a shadow came over him.

It's getting cloudy, he thought. *Perhaps it'll rain and we can go home for tea.*

Suddenly a freak gust of wind lifted his cowboy hat clear off his head.

Pug turned round in surprise only to see the biggest horse he'd EVER seen standing over him. What's more, the horse was eating his hat!

Whoa! Pug took a step back and landed bottom first in a bucket.

The very big horse nuzzled him.

Pug wrinkled his face. He missed Pony.

Thankfully, at that moment, Lady Miranda came back. 'I can't find anyone to sell me a horse –'

She stopped when she saw Pug.

'You clever boy!' she exclaimed. 'You've found me a horse.'

Before Pug knew what was happening she'd scooped him out of

the bucket, grabbed the reins and was attempting to get on the very big horse.

Finally she gave in. 'Give me a leg up, Running Footman Will,' she ordered.

'Are you sure m'Lady?' he asked, looking at Pug's expression.

'Oh Pug'll be fine, won't you, Pug?'

Pug wasn't at all sure he would be.

Lady Miranda gave him a reassuring pat. 'You'll soon earn your spurs,' she told him.

When finally in the saddle, Lady Miranda decided her new steed needed a name.

'I name this horse . . .' she began.

'Erm . . . um . . . I name this horse . . .
Horsey!'

'Excellent choice, m'Lady,' said Running Footman Liam as he picked Pug's hat up off the ground and put it firmly on Pug's head.

'There, Pug, you look just like a cowboy,' Lady Miranda encouraged him.

Pug didn't feel the least bit like a cowboy.

In fact he felt quite dizzy, but before he had a chance to get used to being so high up he realised they were surrounded. There were bandits. Everywhere.

Not now! Pug worried.

'Bandits at quarter past three!' yelled Lady Miranda. 'Giddy up, Horsey!' She flapped her legs wildly against Horsey's sides and he broke into a trot.

Pug bounced up and down in the saddle. For once, he was glad he hadn't had his elevenses. They were going very fast.

Horsey also seemed to have food on his mind because a tempting bag of hay caused him to take a sharp left at the very same moment that Lady Miranda shouted, 'Right!'

During the confusion that followed, Pug noticed a real-life cowboy leaning against a nearby fence.

'Woof!'

Lady Miranda looked over to what had caught Pug's attention.

'Howdy,' said the cowboy. 'The name's – Pah, yuck!' The cowboy spat out a piece of straw that had been hanging from his mouth.

Lady Miranda fell about laughing. 'Pah, yuck! What kind of name is that?'

'No, wait,' said the cowboy. 'My name's not Pah, yuck! My name's Frank. Just Frank.'

'Lady Miranda,' said Lady Miranda, introducing herself. 'And this is Cowboy Pug,' she added.

Pug kept quiet. Was he friend or foe? It was difficult to tell.

'Well, howdy Miss Lady Miranda and Mr Pug. D'you wanna see a card trick?'

'It's Lady Miranda and Cowboy Pug, and no we don't want to see a card trick.'

Frank wasn't prepared for this answer. Who didn't want to see a card trick?

'Go on!' he insisted. 'Pick a card, any card.'

Lady Miranda sighed and pulled a card out of the pack. Pug took a look.

'Don't tell me, don't tell me,' said Frank. 'It's the King of Diamonds!'

'No it's not,' said Lady Miranda.

'Ace of spades!'

'No.'

'Jack of Clubs?'

'No,'

'Um . . .

four of diamonds?'

'Nope.'

Frank scratched his head in bewilderment and Horsey grabbed another mouthful of hay as it tumbled past.

'OK, something else maybe...' Frank changed tack. 'I know, I can make myself disappear in a puff of smoke! D'you wanna see that?'

That sounded better. Pug definitely wanted to see that.

'OK,' replied Lady Miranda.

'Woof!' agreed Pug.

Pleased, Frank spun round and round chanting, 'Alacazam, big frying pan, I'm a rocket man!' At the same time there was a big bang and a teeny weeny puff of smoke. Pug didn't dare look. Horsey bolted straight into the back of a nearby trailer.

And before anyone knew what was happening, a man came along and shut the trailer doors!

'Hey!' shouted Lady Miranda.

'Woof!' said Pug.

But it was too late. The driver started the engine and sped off. They'd been rustled.

Chapter 3

Running Footman Will and Running Footman Liam, who had been busy polishing the sedan chair, came rushing over.

Frank hadn't disappeared (or if he had he'd reappeared very quickly) but Pug, Lady Miranda and Horsey were being driven away!

'Where are they going?' asked Running Footman Will.

'They're going to the county fair,' murmured Frank, feeling a little dazed from his trick. 'Our prize bull, Bert, will be in the show ring later. That's my dad driving,' he added as the trailer headed out of the gates.

'We'd better take you with us,' said Running Footman Will as Running Footman Liam chucked a bucket of cold water over him to stop him

smouldering and put him in the sedan chair.

There was no time to lose. They had to follow that trailer.

As they raced out of the gates there was a distant cry of 'Stop! Thieves!' But since neither Running Footman Will nor Running Footman Liam was aware of having stolen anything they just kept running. After all, you'd be hard pushed to find two more honest people.

After some impressive running

they approached the small market town of Little Witherington. The traffic was terrible.

Frank, who was now feeling much better, was having the time of his life. 'Faster! Faster!' he shouted, leaning out of the window and accidentally clipping a cyclist as he did so. The cyclist wobbled into a grocery stall,

sending watermelons tumbling into the road behind them.

But the running footmen were too busy trying to keep the trailer in sight to notice what was happening.

'I can't see the trailer any more!' Running Footman Will shouted back to Running Footman Liam.

'It's all right,' said Frank. 'It's not far. I know a short cut. Turn left.'

Running Footman Will and Running Footman Liam, used to doing as they were told, took the turning and started heading up a one-way street the wrong way.

An alarming sound followed them.

Nee-naw, nee-naw . . .

'What's that? asked Running Footman Liam, out of breath.

'It's the police!' yelled Frank. 'I think we're being pursued by the law!'

It was indeed the police. Parked in a quiet side street was Maud, Little Witherington's latest police recruit. So far she'd had little to do, this being a law-abiding town, but she was determined that today would be the day she'd make her first arrest.

The rules regarding sedan chairs and one-way streets hadn't actually cropped up in her exam, but Maud was sure that some sort of offence had been committed. She put her foot down, while making sure she went the correct way up the one-way street, as she didn't want to have to arrest herself. This gave the running footmen a bit of a head start. They picked up the pace.

'Oh, you're in BIG trouble now,' said Frank. 'This is so much fun!'

Nee-naw, nee-naw . . .

Despite taking the long way round, Maud was catching up with them.

'Faster! Faster!' shouted Frank.

Meanwhile, Pug, Lady Miranda and Horsey were still stuck in the back of the trailer. Lady Miranda had decided to spend the time practising her lassoing.

Eventually they came to a stop at the Little Witherington County Fair. The driver got out and was rather surprised by what he saw in the back of his trailer.

'Well, I'll be . . .' he exclaimed. 'Is my
Frank's horse holding you hostage or
summut?'

Horsey carried them out of the trailer.

'Frank didn't say this was his horse,' said Lady Miranda. 'I was thinking of buying him.'

'Well,' said Frank's dad, scratching his chin. 'Maybe we can come to an arrangement. Frank doesn't ride him any more, says he's too slow.'

Horsey hung his head.

Pug couldn't believe his ears. Horsey, slow? He'd never been so fast in all his life. Horsey was much quicker than Pony, even on a good day.

'If someone doesn't take him on,' Frank's dad continued, 'we'll have to put him out to pasture.'

Pug immediately felt sorry for Horsey. He knew that Lady Miranda

would never put him out to pasture.
Carefully he put a paw out and stroked
Horsey's mane.

Chapter 4

Lady Miranda arranged to borrow Horsey for the day, as Frank's dad helped untangle them from the lasso. When they were done they shook on the deal, and Pug, Lady Miranda and Horsey were free to enjoy the delights of the Little Witherington County Fair.

Pug had never been to a county fair before. There was a fairground at one end and a showground, where they were giving out prizes for the finest-looking animals, at the other. In the middle was a showjumping arena.

Lady Miranda jumped down and she and Pug led Horsey to the fairground. Horsey nibbled playfully at Pug's tail, which made Pug wag it even more. Now that he was back on solid ground, he could see that Horsey wasn't scary at all. In fact, Pug was beginning to like him very much.

Lady Miranda was clearly an expert at fairgrounds. Pug was always amazed by how much she knew. She showed them the High Striker,

and then, for a treat, they went for some candyfloss.

In the Hall of Mirrors Horsey felt ten years younger, while Pug worried that Lady Miranda was right – his eyes really were bigger than his stomach.

At the Runaway Train Lady Miranda had to negotiate with the fairground attendant. Pug waited patiently. He was just beginning to get the feeling that being a cowboy wasn't so bad after all when, to his horror,

the Runaway Train started heading
straight for him! The train's whistle
blew. The passengers screamed.
Pug was so frightened he closed his
eyes . . .

'PUUUUUUUUG!' screamed Lady Miranda.

Pug opened his eyes to find that he was flying! Horsey had grabbed Pug in his mouth just as the Runaway Train thundered past him.

'Oh, Horsey, you're a hero!' said Lady Miranda. 'I shall love you forever!'

Horsey didn't know what to do with all this praise. He shyly looked at his hooves.

Lady Miranda placed Pug on Horsey's back. They decided it was probably a good time to leave the fairground and head back towards the showground. In the main arena a showjumping competition was underway.

Just as Lady Miranda was chatting to an official with a clipboard, Running Footman Will, Running Footman Liam and Frank came into view.

'We've been having the best time!' Frank shouted.

Running Footman Will and Running Footman Liam looked pretty exhausted to Pug. He was just wondering if they might need a snack when Maud the police officer drove up.

'You two,' she said, pointing at Running Footman Will and Running Footman Liam. 'I'm arresting you for travelling up a one-way street the wrong way!'

'You can't arrest them!' said an indignant Lady Miranda. 'I won't allow it.'

Just then a rather red-faced woman on a bicycle stepped in. 'No, Officer, arrest that girl, she's stolen our horse!'

Everyone turned to look at Lady Miranda.

'I can explain everything!' she assured them.

'Step this way, Miss,' Maud told Lady Miranda.

'Pug!' Lady Miranda called out. Pug gave a low growl from his place on Horsey's back.

'Mum, it's all right,' said Frank. 'This is Lady Miranda. She's a friend. And the running footmen went up the one-way street the wrong way because of me.'

'You keep quiet,' said Frank's mum. 'I'll deal with you later.'

In all the commotion no one noticed the ring steward patting Horsey on the rump. 'You're up next,' he said, and Horsey trotted into the main arena.

Chapter 5

Pug and Horsey entered the arena to a polite round of applause.

'Ladies and gentlemen,' said the commentator, looking at his notes. 'This is our final pair of the afternoon: Horsey and his rider, whose name I don't have . . .'

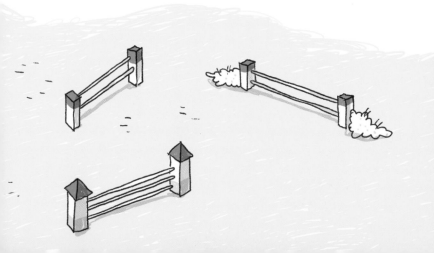

'Cowboy Pug!' shouted Lady Miranda from the stand. She'd managed to smooth things over with Police Officer Maud and Frank's mum.

'Thank you, Miss. Please take your seats – the round is about to begin.'

Lady Miranda and Frank, feeling like they'd been in enough trouble for one day, quickly sat down.

Horsey had been munching on some flowers decorating one of the jumps, but when he saw Frank it gave him an idea. He'd show Frank he wasn't so slow after all.

The steward's whistle blew.

'The time to beat is one minute twelve seconds,' the commentator informed the crowd. 'Let's see what these two can do.'

Pug gingerly wriggled round in the saddle so that he was facing the right way. Horsey picked up his hooves in a manner he hadn't done since he was a young colt and cantered towards the first fence.

Pug could not believe it, nor could the crowd.

'Safely over the first,' said the commentator.

The next jump was a triple.

One . . .

Two . . .

Three!

The crowd were on their feet. They'd never seen anything quite like it.

Horsey gave Pug a nudge to make sure he was securely in the saddle.

'Astonishing!' the commentator cheered, wiping his glasses. He couldn't believe what he was seeing. 'Only one more jump to go – the water.'

The water?! thought Pug. *Oh, no!* Pug didn't like water.

In his fear, Pug went to take an extra big bite of Horsey's mane and dug his claws in to hold on. The shock spurred Horsey on and he sailed over the water jump like a true champion.

'Hor-sey!

Hor-sey! Hor-sey!'

cheered the crowd, who were on their feet.

Horsey's nose crossed the finish line.

'One minute thirteen seconds! We've never seen a round like that before!'

The crowd went wild. Never had a team in second place been so popular.

Lady Miranda and Frank rushed into the arena to congratulate them.

Police Officer Maud had forgotten her disappointment at not being able to make an arrest.

Frank's mum kissed Frank, which was quite embarrassing.

Running Footman Will and Running Footman Liam lifted Pug up on to their shoulders so everyone could see him.

'Cow-boy Pug! Cow-boy Pug! Cow-boy Pug!' they cheered.

The medal ceremony was very moving. Horsey received a nice rosette and Pug was given a shiny silver medal.

After the photographs Frank patted Horsey. 'You're not so slow after all, are you?'

Horsey whinnied and then playfully swiped Frank's cowboy hat off his head. He did love hats.

Pug thought he'd burst with pride. *Well done Horsey*, he thought. But his thoughts were interrupted by an urgent cry.

'Stop! Thief!'

Chapter 6

'They've stolen Bert!' shouted Frank's dad.

Running Footman Will gave Lady Miranda a leg up and she joined Pug in the saddle. 'Chaaaarge!' she shouted as Horsey galloped after the trailer.

They caught up quickly and Lady Miranda leaped out of the saddle and on to the back of the trailer as it sped along. Unfortunately, her sleeve caught on the bolt of the door and it unfastened. The door swung open but Lady Miranda clung on.

Inside the trailer Bert the Bull looked angry. Steam was coming from his nostrils. He pawed the ground, snorted and then charged out of the back of the trailer.

The bandit driving the truck looked back to see what had happened.

'Look where you're going!' the other one shouted as they crashed into a stack of hay bales.

'You're nicked!' shouted Police Officer Maud triumphantly. Finally she'd made an arrest.

But the drama hadn't finished yet. Terrible screams were coming from the tea tent. Bert was on the rampage! Tea drinkers were scattering and running for their lives!

'Woof!' said Pug.

Horsey knew immediately what he meant. He galloped towards the tea tent. As Horsey rushed towards Bert, Pug took the lasso in his mouth and flung it through the air.

It landed perfectly around Bert's neck.

Pug jumped from the saddle and walked up to Bert.

Bert eyed Pug suspiciously.

Pug could hear Bert's breathing, and his own heart was racing.

Bert was angry and Bert was big.

The crowd looked on.

No one dared say a thing.

And then Pug had an idea.

Slowly, and very carefully, he walked over to a nearby upturned tea trolley. After careful inspection he grabbed a Victoria sponge in his mouth.

A ribbon of drool fell from Bert's lips.

Pug bravely dropped the cake at Bert's feet.

Bert sniffed it.

Then he tucked in!

Frank's dad grabbed the lasso. 'I'll take it from here,' he said. 'I've never seen anyone catch Bert so quickly. You're a natural.'

'Oh Pug, you're a true cowboy,' exclaimed Lady Miranda.

'That was amazing!' said Frank, and he offered Horsey a sugar lump.

'These are for you,' he added, pulling a bunch of flowers from his sleeve and offering them to Lady Miranda.

'Thank you,' she blushed, 'but it was all Pug really.'

Pug gave her a big puggy kiss.

Back at No. 10, The Crescent, Pug and Lady Miranda settled down to tea. Wendy had made a fresh batch of jam tarts: Pug's favourite.

Running Footman Will and Running Footman Liam were mucking out Pony's stable.

'Did you find a suitable horse, m'Lady?' asked Wendy as she handed Pony a carrot.

'Well,' replied Lady Miranda between mouthfuls, 'Frank decided that he actually quite liked Horsey and I didn't want to split them up. Besides, I'm not sure being a cowboy is all it's cracked up to be.'

She looked at Pug adoringly. 'I won't ever make you a cowboy again,' she whispered in his ear. 'I don't think all that hay is good for you.'

Pug sighed contentedly. He liked being at home.

Lady Miranda gave him a little pat. 'You're such a good boy,' she said.

Pug wagged his curly tail.

'I'll just have to think of something else you can be instead.'

A Letter from the Author

Howdy Partner!

I hope you've enjoyed reading about Pug's adventures as a cowboy. He can be a reluctant hero at times, and left to his own devices he'd probably plump for an afternoon on the sofa, tucking in to a fresh batch of Wendy's famous jam tarts.

Thankfully, Pug has Lady Miranda on hand to encourage him to discover the big wide world. She makes sure he doesn't miss out on all the fun. Pug would do anything for Lady Miranda and she'd be lost without him.

A good friend will encourage us to do the best we can, make us brave when we feel afraid and take us on adventures we never thought possible. It just remains to be seen where Pug's friendship with Lady Miranda will take him next!

Happy reading.

With love,

Laura x

© Red Rabbit Photography

JOIN **PUG** ON HIS THIRD ADVENTURE IN

SAFARI PUG

COMING NOVEMBER 2017

READ **PUG'S** FIRST ADVENTURE

CAPTAIN PUG

AVAILABLE NOW

Laura James's love of storytelling began at an early age and led her to study Film and Writing for Young People at Bath Spa University. The adventures of Pug are based on the antics of her very own adventurous dogs, Brian and Florence. Laura lives in the West Country.

Églantine Ceulemans was born in Belgium where she spent her childhood devouring comics before moving to France to study illustration. As well as drawing, she loves riding her blue bicycle, cooking (which she is not very good at) and cleaning windows (which she is very good at). Églantine lives in Lyon, France.